Equipped to Serve

# Volunteer Youth Worker Training Course

VOLUNTEER HANDBOOK

# YOUTH SPECIALTIES TITLES

## Professional Resources
The Church and the American Teenager (previously released as Growing Up in America)
Developing Spiritual Growth in Junior High Students
Feeding Your Forgotten Soul
Help! I'm a Sunday School Teacher!
Help! I'm a Volunteer Youth Worker!
High School Ministry
How to Recruit and Train Volunteer Youth Workers (previously released as Unsung Heroes)
Junior High Ministry (Revised Edition)
The Ministry of Nurture
Organizing Your Youth Ministry
Peer Counseling in Youth Groups
Advanced Peer Counseling in Youth Groups
The Youth Minister's Survival Guide
Youth Ministry Nuts and Bolts

## Discussion Starter Resources
Amazing Tension Getters
Get 'Em Talking
High School TalkSheets
Junior High TalkSheets
High School TalkSheets: Psalms and Proverbs
Junior High TalkSheets: Psalms and Proverbs
More High School TalkSheets
More Junior High TalkSheets
Option Plays
Parent Ministry TalkSheets
Tension Getters
Tension Getters Two

## Ideas Library
Ideas Combo 1-4, 5-8, 9-12, 13-16, 17-20, 21-24, 25-28, 29-32, 33-36, 37-40, 41-44, 45-48, 49-52, 53, 54
Ideas Index

## Youth Ministry Programming
Adventure Games
Creative Bible Lessons
Creative Programming Ideas for Junior High Ministry
Creative Socials and Special Events
Equipped to Serve
Facing Your Future
Good Clean Fun
Good Clean Fun, Volume 2
Great Fundraising Ideas for Youth Groups
Great Games for City Kids
Great Ideas for Small Youth Groups
Great Retreats for Youth Groups
Greatest Skits on Earth
Greatest Skits on Earth, Volume 2
Holiday Ideas for Youth Groups (Revised Edition)
Hot Illustrations for Youth Talks
Hot Talks
Junior High Game Nights
More Junior High Game Nights
On-Site: 40 On-Location Youth Programs

Play It! Great Games for Groups
Play It Again! More Great Games for Groups
Road Trip
Super Sketches for Youth Ministry
Teaching the Bible Creatively
Teaching the Truth about Sex
Up Close and Personal: How to Build Community in Your Youth Group

## 4th-6th Grade Ministry
Attention Grabbers for 4th-6th Graders
4th-6th Grade TalkSheets
Great Games for 4th-6th Graders
How to Survive Middle School
Incredible Stories
More Attention Grabbers for 4th-6th Graders
More Great Games for 4th-6th Graders
Quick and Easy Activities for 4th-6th Graders
More Quick and Easy Activities for 4th-6th Graders
Teach 'Toons

## Clip Art
ArtSource Volume 1—Fantastic Activities
ArtSource Volume 2—Borders, Symbols, Holidays, and Attention Getters
ArtSource Volume 3—Sports
ArtSource Volume 4—Phrases and Verses
ArtSource Volume 5—Amazing Oddities and Appalling Images
ArtSource Volume 6—Spiritual Topics
Youth Specialties Clip Art Book
Youth Specialties Clip Art Book, Volume 2

## Video
Edge TV
God Views
The Heart of Youth Ministry: A Morning with Mike Yaconelli
Next Time I Fall in Love Video Curriculum
Promo Spots for Junior High Game Nights
Resource Seminar Video Series
Understanding Your Teenage Video Curriculum
Witnesses

## Student Books
Going the Distance
Good Advice
Grow for It Journal
Grow for It Journal: Through the Scriptures
How to Live with Your Parents without Losing Your Mind
I Don't Remember Dropping the Skunk, But I Do Remember Trying to Breathe
Next Time I Fall in Love
Next Time I Fall in Love Journal
101 Things to Do During a Dull Sermon

Equipped to Serve

# Volunteer
# Youth Worker
# Training
# Course

VOLUNTEER HANDBOOK

Youth
Specialties

ZondervanPublishingHouse
Grand Rapids, Michigan
A Division of HarperCollins Publishers

Equipped to Serve: Youth Specialties' Volunteer Youth Worker Training Course
Volunteer Handbook
Copyright ©1994 by Youth Specialties, Inc.

Youth Specialties Books, 1224 Greenfield Drive, El Cajon, California 92021, are published by Zondervan Publishing House, 5300 Patterson, S.E., Grand Rapids, Michigan 49530.

Edited by Noel Becchetti and Lorraine Triggs
Typography and design by Patton Brothers Design
Cover illustration by Court Patton

Printed in the United States of America

98 99 / MAL / 8 7

# TABLE OF CONTENTS

# ACKNOWLEDGEMENTS

I am grateful to my wife, Sue, who has been with me through the journey of youth ministry, and to my staff at Youth Leadership, who are superb co-workers.

My passion to train volunteers and my belief in their value comes from a caring adult who had the courage to step out of his world and meet for breakfast with a confused teenager. And so, this book is dedicated to a simple man named Bob Hagstrom. Thanks Bob.

Dennis "Tiger" McLuen

# INTRODUCTION

I began in youth ministry over twenty-one years ago as a young college student who said "yes" when asked to be a volunteer in a youth ministry program. I knew nothing about the job and the expectations. I knew nothing about youth ministry and of the skills I needed to be effective. I just thought it would be fun to be involved and I knew that I would grow from the experience.

In the years since that experience, I have grown in many ways, learned some new things, and, hopefully, gained a few more skills. But the one constant has been my enthusiasm for this thing called youth ministry. I am excited about the opportunity to share the good news of the Gospel with teenagers, and to help adult volunteers become effective youth leaders.

This training course actually started years ago as I tried to equip my volunteer leaders with skills as well as motivate them for this exciting task of youth ministry. It has been developed more recently in my work with Youth Leadership. YL started a quarterly volunteer training series five years ago, and it has become one of my favorite things to do. I love to be at these sessions with volunteers who are giving valuable time to serve young people. I am excited to now be a part of your ministry to teenagers.

I write this training course as an instructor in youth ministry and as a volunteer youth worker. In my home church, I am a leader of a small group of high school guys and also help out in the senior high ministry when time allows. My hope is that this material will be encouraging and helpful to all of us who volunteer our time with teenagers.

My hope is that *Equipped to Serve* will
- Encourage you in the valuable role you play in the lives of teenagers
- Equip you with valuable skills needed for effective ministry
- Help you to better understand teenagers
- Build community within your leadership team
- Create an opportunity for you to develop specific action steps for your ministry
- Give you a vision for the great opportunity you have to change kids' lives for the Kingdom

This handbook will become a reference point for you as you record your insights, thoughts, and perceptions. This is your resource—bring it to each meeting as you learn, grow, and become better equipped to serve teenagers.

God bless you as you serve!

Dennis "Tiger" McLuen

# You
# Are
# Valuable

SESSION ONE

# Let's Get Acquainted

**1** Describe yourself, your situation in life (married, single, etc.), and what you do (work, school, etc.).

**2** What do you like to do best with your free time?

**3** When you play competitive games (from Monopoly to sports), you usually:
    a. Get bored
    b. Get into an argument
    c. Cheat
    d. Hang in there to the bitter end
    e. Have fun no matter what
    f. Win at all costs

**4** Share a favorite childhood vacation memory:

**5** Why did you come to this meeting?
    a. I was asked to come and couldn't say no
    b. I have friends who are here
    c. I am curious
    d. I have past experience in youth ministry
    e. I want to help the youth
    f. I'm not sure
    g. Other: _____

# Fears and Worries: Past and Present

Complete this sheet, then share your answers and comments with the others in your group.

**1** **Write down two or three fears or worries that you had as a junior higher:**

**2** **What is one accomplishment you achieved as a teenager that you feel good about?**

**3** **On the following scale, put an X to mark your "worry quotient" as an adolescent:**

| No worries | Pretty relaxed | Up and down | High tension |

**4** **What are some of your fears or worries as you think about working with young people this year in youth ministry?**

# NOTES

# NOTES

# NOTES

# NOTES

# Know Your Audience

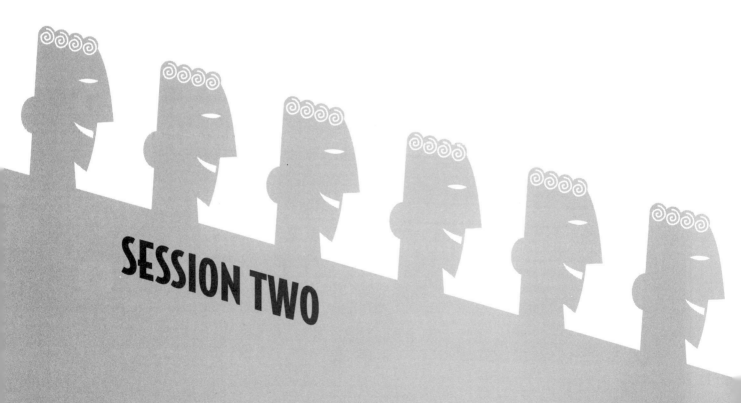

SESSION TWO

## Resource Sheet A

# The Adolescent Audience— A People Who Are:

■ **In transition—physically, emotionally, socially, mentally, spiritually**
Teens are moving from childhood to adulthood in *all* areas of their lives.

■ **Under influence**
From the media, music, parents, school, peers, the future, and the changing world.

■ **Developing an identity**
Teens desire to gain their own identity separate from parents, teachers, and churches.

■ **Relational in perspective**
The world of the teenager is oriented around relationships or the lack of relationships.

■ **Struggling with their families**
Many teens struggle with how their lives intersect (or collide) with those of their families'.

■ **Changing the way they think**
Teens operate in a visual world and seek immediate results and connections.

■ **Reflecting adult society**
Teenagers often mirror our adult culture back to us in painful ways.

■ **Losing hope**
Growing numbers of teens are feeling more and more hopeless.

■ **Feeling driven**
The average teen can be a roller coaster of emotions.

# Know Your Audience

How well do you know the teenage world? Let's find out.

Circle your answers:

**1** **When I think about the "teenage world," I feel like:**
   a. A visitor from another planet.
   b. I haven't studied for the test in class.
   c. I can recognize a teenager.
   d. I know some basic information about adolescence.
   e. I should be teaching this session.

**2** **In terms of knowing specific teens:**
   a. I don't even know where the youth room is.
   b. I don't know any teenagers on a first-name basis.
   c. I know a few kids in this church.
   d. I have a pretty good sense of the kids in this ministry and some of their issues.
   e. I hang out with kids all the time and scare my adult friends.

**3** **When it comes to knowing teenage culture:**
   a. I am clueless—I don't know MTV from M&M's.
   b. I lost touch sometime after the disco craze.
   c. I can recognize the music as I scan by it on my car radio.
   d. I am up on it, but it usually is going by me too quickly.
   e. I am young, hip, and groovy. I know all the lingo and can really connect with kids.

Now, write your answers to the following:

**4** **How can I find out more about the world of the teenager?**

**5** **How can I get to know some specific teenagers in this church?**

**6** **How do I see culture affecting the teenagers in our church and community?**

**7** **How do I see the basic needs to be loved, to be valuable, and to be connected expressed in the teenagers in this church?**

# Categories of Teenagers

Think about the teenagers in this church or ministry, and the needs that they may have. We will use the categories described on the video to help us to think together about the audience. The definitions of each of these categories are explained on page 23 of this Worksheet. If you have a particular area of responsibility (Sunday school, small groups, etc.) then use this Worksheet for your area only.

| Category of teen | Teens who may fit here | Possible needs of these teens |
|---|---|---|
| Uninterested | Lindsay Pen mike | Knowledge |
| Attending Resister | | |
| Status Quo | | |
| Seeker | | |
| Committed | | |

## Uninterested

These teenagers are not interested in spiritual things. They usually don't attend youth activities and may be cynical about such things. These young people have questions about life and faith, but tend to think that church and the Bible have no connection to their world.

## Attending Resister

These teenagers do attend some or all of your activities, but are there under duress. They are usually pressured to come by their parents and they have little interest in what is happening in the youth ministry. They may be passive in their resistance (apathy, non-involvement) or they may be active (negative, interrupting, sarcastic).

## Status Quo

These teens attend youth activities, and may in fact be very consistent. They react with a variety of levels of enthusiasm to the activities, but the key issue for these adolescents is that they do not want church, God, or the Bible to affect their lives in significant ways. Their primary goal in life is to stay the same as the rest of their friends. All adolescents demonstrate this quality at various times, but these teens are focused in not wanting to change. They state belief in God, but have no interest in anything that may challenge them.

## Seeker

These teens are starting to ask questions and seek out spiritual things. They are more attentive in class and may talk to you individually. Their attendance may not be consistent, depending on their families, and what category they were in before entering this stage. Yet these adolescents are open to wondering what a life lived for God would look like.

## Committed

These teens are serious about their faith and are trying to live it out in their world. They are at different levels of Bible knowledge, and have a variety of personality types, but these teens want to live for God. They can get bored with pat answers, with being spectators, and with having no leadership roles. They want to try new things, be stretched, and get involved.

# NOTES

# NOTES

# NOTES

# NOTES

# NOTES

# Hitting Your Target

**SESSION THREE**

# Setting Our Ministry Goals

**1** What are one or two reactions you have to what Tiger and Mike had to say?

**2** What do you think are the benefits to having goals in youth ministry?

**3** Now, fill in your personal goals and hopes for the youth ministry program.

**Your Ministry Target Area (e.g., Junior high, 10th grade girls, etc.):**

_____

**I.** What would you like your students to KNOW this year?
(e.g., the Bible, family information, denominational doctrine, etc.)

**II.** What would you like your students to be able to DO this year?
(e.g., skiing, hayrides, progressive dinners, etc.)

**III.** What would you like your students to EXPERIENCE this year?
(e.g., feeling valued, experiencing worship in a personal way,
being cared for by a peer, etc.)

**IV.** What would you like them to BECOME this year?
(e.g., able to make healthier decisions, a person more focused on
Christ, etc.)

# Programming Windows

This chart will help you look at where (and how) your programs can be placed. Each window is an opportunity to program an event or activity to help you accomplish your goals. These windows are the most common ones, although you may have some variations. It is important to note that each window can impact the others. The things you do in one window may improve, or cause difficulties in, the other windows. For example, a retreat in special events may help you in your Sunday morning window. Using this Programming Windows chart, list some program examples for each window:

| Sunday Morning | Midweek Activity |
|---|---|
| | |
| **Special Events** | **Personal Relationships** |
| | |

## Extra Credit

Go back to Worksheet 2.1. Which categories of teens usually attend certain windows? Do the programs these kids attend meet the needs of those kids? Why or why not?

# NOTES

# NOTES

# NOTES

# How to Develop Healthy Relationships with Teens

## SESSION FOUR

# Relational Ministry on a Busy Schedule

" . . . the foundation of youth ministry is relational ministry, not the ministry of teaching. Where the ministry of teaching is primary, young people will tend to resist it. Where the ministry of friendship is primary, the ministry of teaching can make progress."
Michael Warren, *Youth and the Future of the Church*, 1982, Seabury Press

Each person brings a different personality style to relational ministry. Some of us are energized by groups of people, while others of us prefer quiet, one-to-one relationships. Some of us always follow a plan, while others of us are spontaneous and free-flowing. Some of us state our opinions quickly and easily, while others of us listen more and have difficulty articulating our thoughts.

There is no one right relational style. God wants you to use the personality that he has given you to reach out to teenagers. This Worksheet will help you respond to the idea of relational youth ministry and to the information from Video Segment Number Five.

**1** **How do you best get to know others? What style seems to work best for you? Put an X on the line that best fits you when you think of relating to teens:**

Introvert————————————————————————Extrovert
Quiet————————————————————————————Noisy
Ask questions————————————————————Give opinions
Behind the scenes————————————————————Up front
Planner————————————————————————Spontaneous
Homebody————————————————————————Let's go out

**2** **How have you seen relational ministry work out specifically in your life and the lives of others? (Feel free to include examples from outside youth ministry.)**

**3** **Set your personal relational ministry goals, using the formula of one hour and thirty minutes per week given in the video:**

Ten minutes:two phone calls

Twenty minutes:three written notes

One hour:one personal contact—individual or small group

a. Time per week/month I will give to building relationships with teenagers:

b. Specific teens I will focus on in the next six months:

c. Specific steps I will take with those teens:

1.

2.

3.

4.

Note: These specific goals are a way to clarify your hopes and are not meant to weigh you down. If you're having trouble coming up with goals, discuss it with your small group and/or your group leader.

# How to Build Healthy Relationships with Teens

- Listen.

- Learn names.

- Show an interest in teens' lives.

- Accept kids as they are.

- Develop a sense of humor.

- Attend events that teens are involved in.

- Initiate, even though it may feel strange.

- Speak naturally and conversationally.

- Be yourself.

- Pray for those kids you are getting to know.

- Communicate your enthusiasm rather than flaunt your doubt.

- Don't force yourself into situations.

- Be prepared to have to earn the right to be heard.

- Be sensitive to boundaries of time, physical contact, emotions, and differences in maturity.

# NOTES

# NOTES

# NOTES

# How To Lead A Small Group

**SESSION FIVE**

# Small-Group Flashback

**1** Describe a positive experience you had in a small group as a leader or participant. What was it like? What made the group effective?

**2** Now, describe a negative experience you had in a small group as a leader or participant. What was it like?

**3** What were the differences between the two groups that made the one group go well and the other one struggle?

**4** How do you feel about leading a small group? What do you look forward to? What do you fear?

**5** Place an X on the line that reflects your feelings about leading a small-group Bible study/discussion:

panic-stricken      nervous          fair          pretty relaxed      very cool

# The Small-Group Lab

One person in your small group will be your leader for the next fifteen to twenty minutes. They will lead a discussion on one of the following topics. Please participate fully in the discussion and then record your observations afterwards.

**Leader:** Facilitate a discussion on one of the topics listed below. Use whatever style feels most comfortable as you get your group to discuss this subject. Stop the group in twenty minutes.

Topics (choose one):
1. **Moments when you felt closest to God**
2. **The joys and struggles of parenting**
3. **A painful time in your life as a child**
4. **Why you are involved in youth ministry**
5. **Some of your goals for life**

**Participants only** complete the following:

**1. The leader did the following things to help the discussion:**

**2. The leader could have been even more effective by:**

**3. What seemed to be most difficult for the leader?**

**4. What seemed to be most comfortable for the leader?**

**5. The leader seemed (place an X on the line):**

Nervous _____Comfortable

**6. The conversation flowed (place an X on the line):**

With difficulty_____Easily

**Leader only** complete the following:

**1. Please mark an X on each scale to indicate how you felt during the exercise:**

Nervous _____Calm

Self-conscious _____Focused on group

**2. The most difficult part of this exercise was:**

**3. The part that felt the most comfortable for me was:**

**4. From this exercise, I learned:**

# Survival Ideas for Small Groups

(Adapted with permission from *The Youth Builder*, Jim Burns, 1988, Harvest House)

- Include everyone whenever possible.
- At the beginning, get everyone in the group to talk.
- Four in a group is best; six is okay; eight should be the maximum.
- Be aware of new people and include them in the conversation.
- Remember that small groups often raise the tension level (because people can't hide).
- Move from light to heavy discussion.
- Ask "I feel" rather than "I know" questions.
- The longer the group is together, the better they will feel about the group.
- In a small group it's easier to share, pray, encourage, and be personal.
- Prepare your discussion questions and vary how you ask them.
- Avoid any put-downs.
- Discussion questions should be answerable.
- Allow people the right to pass and not share.
- Create a casual and relaxed atmosphere.
- Don't always expound on the answer yourself.
- Call people by name.
- Eye contact and body language are important for the leader.
- When you ask someone to read, make sure he/she is able to read out loud or else don't ask.
- Get your group in a comfortable atmosphere where everyone can see each other's eyes.
- Request confidentiality in the group.

## An effective small-group leader:

- Guides the discussion with control and flexibility
- Encourages as much participation as possible
- Asks a variety of questions that involve the group
- Listens well
- Arranges seating to involve participants
- Models the skills he/she wants to develop in group members
- Notices the people in the room, the conversations occurring, and the non-verbal signals
- Creates an inviting, positive atmosphere
- Affirms the ideas expressed by group members
- Doesn't panic with silence
- Doesn't let one person monopolize the discussion

# NOTES

# NOTES

# NOTES

# Caring Skills 101

SESSION SIX

# The Ministry of Listening

*"Everyone should be quick to listen, slow to speak"* (James 1:19)

## 🌐 ATTITUDES in Effective Listening 🌐

Be sincere. Don't try to fake good listening—it won't work. Take the time to listen properly.

Accept the other person and his or her feelings. Good listening begins with acceptance.

Trust in the person's capacity to handle his or her feelings, and have confidence in his or her ability to work at solutions. Trust in the Lord to work with this person.

Active listening does not solve problems. It creates an environment conducive to problem solving.

## 🌐 GUIDELINES for Effective Listening 🌐

Identify the CONTENT in the message. What is being said? React to what is being presented, not the way it is presented.

Figure out the FEELINGS in the messages. How does the person feel about what he or she is saying? Try to see and feel the situation through that person's eyes, not your own.

FEEDBACK what you are hearing. Do this without judgment or without sending back a message of your own. Share both the content and the feelings that you are hearing.

Try to paraphrase what the other person has said. Condense it down to a sentence or two. Listen for themes that you are observing. Begin your sentences with a short introduction:

> "You feel that . . . "
> "What I am hearing you say is . . . "
> "You're (name the feeling) . . . "
> "So, it's kinda like . . . "

Practice, Practice, Practice

Practice some more!

# Counseling and Caring Skills

## Six Key Questions for the Helper

**1** Why am I here?

**2** What do I have to offer this person?

**3** What does this person need?

**4** What are my limits as a helper?

**5** How long can I offer this to this person?

## Seven Danger Areas in Counseling

**1 The Question-Answer Trap**
We don't really listen; we just focus on asking questions.
Be careful of how many questions you ask.

**2 The Messiah Complex**
Since the teen has talked to us, we can "rescue" him or her.

**3 The Bible Bullet Syndrome**
We slide into easy answers with a Bible verse tagged on.
Caring for people is bringing them into contact with the Great Physician,
but it is not always filled with easy answers.

**4 The Helping = Fixing Mentality**
If we are to help people, we must fix their problems.

**5 The "Counseling Others to Meet Our Needs" Syndrome**
We care for others in order to meet our own needs. We must not counsel
out of curiosity, a need for power, a need for relationships, or out of guilt.

**6 The No-Weaknesses Weakness**
Every counselor has certain limitations and weaknesses. This is only
dangerous when we won't admit them.

**7 The Boundary Violation**
Our job is to work within the boundaries of other people, and not
impose our expectations on them.

# Three Reasons to Refer a Counselee

## Time Limits
We don't have the time it takes to work through the issues presented to us.

## Competence Limits
The level of expertise needed to deal with the issues presented to us is more than we can offer.

## Emotional Limits
The subject or issue presented is inappropriate for us.

See your youth pastor or pastor for a list of local referral sources you can utilize when it's time for you to withdraw from the counseling process.

# NOTES

# NOTES

# NOTES

# NOTES

# NOTES